Dear Parent:
Your child's love of reading starts here!

Every child learns to read in a different way and at his or her own speed. Some go back and forth between reading levels and read favorite books again and again. Others read through each level in order. You can help your young reader improve and become more confident by encouraging his or her own interests and abilities. From books your child reads with you to the first books he or she reads alone, there are I Can Read Books for every stage of reading:

SHARED READING
Basic language, word repetition, and whimsical illustrations, ideal for sharing with your emergent reader

BEGINNING READING
Short sentences, familiar words, and simple concepts for children eager to read on their own

READING WITH HELP
Engaging stories, longer sentences, and language play for developing readers

READING ALONE
Complex plots, challenging vocabulary, and high-interest topics for the independent reader

ADVANCED READING
Short paragraphs, chapters, and exciting themes for the perfect bridge to chapter books

I Can Read Books have introduced children to the joy of reading since 1957. Featuring award-winning authors and illustrators and a fabulous cast of beloved characters, I Can Read Books set the standard for beginning readers.

A lifetime of discovery begins with the magical words "I Can Read!"

Visit www.icanread.com for information
on enriching your child's reading experience.

Biscuit
Finds a Friend

story by ALYSSA SATIN CAPUCILLI
pictures by PAT SCHORIES

HarperCollins*Publishers*

HarperCollins®, ☛®, and I Can Read Book® are trademarks of HarperCollins Publishers Inc.

www.harperchildrens.com
Library of Congress Cataloging-in-Publication Data
Capucilli, Alyssa.
    Biscuit finds a friend / story by Alyssa Satin Capucilli ; pictures by Pat Schories.
      p.   cm. — (A my first I can read book)
    Summary: A puppy helps a little duck find its way home to the pond.
    ISBN-10: 0-06-027412-3 (trade bdg.) — ISBN-13: 978-0-06-027412-2 (trade bdg.)
    ISBN-10: 0-06-027413-1 (lib. bdg.) — ISBN-13: 978-0-06-027413-9 (lib. bdg.)
    ISBN-10: 0-06-444243-8 (pbk.) — ISBN-13: 978-0-06-444243-5 (pbk.)
    [1. Dogs—Fiction. 2. Ducks—Fiction.] I. Schories, Pat, ill. II. Title. III. Series.
PZ7.C179Bis 1997   96-18368
[E]—dc20   CIP
                                                                                                                      AC

For two very special friends,
Margaret Jean O'Connor and Willie Hornick.

Woof! Woof!

What has Biscuit found?

Is it a ball?

Woof!

Is it a bone?

Woof!

Quack!

It is a little duck.

The little duck is lost.

Woof! Woof!

We will bring
the little duck
back to the pond.

Woof! Woof!

Here, little duck.
Here is the pond.

Here are your mother
and your father.
Quack!

Here are your brothers
and your sisters.
Quack! Quack!

14

The ducks say thank you.
Thank you for finding
the little duck.

Quack!
The little duck
wants to play.

Quack!
Woof!

Quack!
Woof!

Splash!

Biscuit fell into the pond!

Silly Biscuit.

You are all wet!

Woof!

Oh no, Biscuit.

Not a big shake!

Woof!

Time to go home, Biscuit.

Quack! Quack!

Say good-bye, Biscuit.

Woof! Woof!

Good-bye, little duck.

Biscuit has found
a new friend.